Harriet,
You'll Drive Me Wild!

BY MEM FOX

ILLUSTRATED BY MARLA FRAZEE

VOYAGER BOOKS · HARCOURT, INC.

SAN DIEGO   NEW YORK   LONDON

To Wendy Bean, the Soft-Voice Queen
—MEM FOX

To my sister, Janel—transplendent amidst the Legos
—MARLA FRAZEE

www.HarcourtBooks.com

First Voyager Books edition 2003
Voyager Books is a trademark of Harcourt, Inc., registered in the
United States of America and/or other jurisdictions.

The Library of Congress has cataloged the hardcover edition as follows:
Fox, Mem, 1946–
Harriet, you'll drive me wild!/Mem Fox; illustrated by Marla Frazee.
p. cm.
Summary: When a young girl has a series of mishaps at home one Saturday,
her mother tries not to lose her temper—and does not quite succeed.
[1. Mothers and daughters—Fiction. 2. Clumsiness—Fiction.
3. Temper—Fiction.] I. Frazee, Marla, ill. II. Title.
PZ7.F8373Har 2000
[E]—dc21   98-11697
ISBN 0-15-201977-4
ISBN 0-15-204598-8 pb

H G F E

The illustrations in this book were done in pencil and
transparent drawing inks on Strathmore paper, hot press finish.
The display type was set in Minion Swash italic.
The text type was set in Adobe Caslon.
Color separations by Bright Arts Ltd., Hong Kong
Manufactured by South China Printing Company, Ltd., China
Production supervision by Sandra Grebenar and Wendi Taylor
Designed by Kaelin Chappell and Marla Frazee

*H*arriet Harris was a pesky child.
She didn't mean to be. She just was.

One morning at breakfast, she knocked over a glass of juice, just like that.

Her mother didn't like to yell, so instead she said,
"Harriet, my *darling* child."
"I'm sorry," said Harriet, and she was.

At snacktime, she dribbled jam all over her jeans, just like that.

Her mother didn't like to yell, so instead she said,
"Harriet, my *darling* child. Harriet, you'll drive me wild."
"I'm sorry," said Harriet, and she was.

Before lunch, when Harriet was painting a picture, she dripped paint onto the carpet, just like that.

Her mother didn't like to yell, so instead she said,
"Harriet, my *darling* child. Harriet, you'll drive me wild.
Harriet, sweetheart, what are we to do?"
"I'm sorry," said Harriet, and she was.

At lunch, Harriet slid off her chair and the tablecloth came with her, just like that.

Her mother didn't like to yell, so instead she said,
"Harriet, my *darling* child. Harriet, you'll drive me wild.
Harriet, sweetheart, what are we to do?
Harriet Harris, I'm talking to *you*."
"I'm sorry," said Harriet, and she was.

Later that afternoon, when Harriet was meant to be napping, she ripped open a pillow, just like that.

$\mathcal{A}$ thousand feathers flew in every direction.

There was a terrible silence.

Then Harriet's mother began to yell.
She yelled and yelled and yelled.

"I'm sorry," Harriet cried. "I'm really, really sorry."

*H*er mother took a deep breath.

"I know you are," she said, hugging Harriet tight.

"I'm sorry, too. I shouldn't have yelled, and I wish I hadn't.

But sometimes it happens, just like that."

"Big mess," said Harriet.

"A *very* big mess," said her mother.

And she started to laugh.

*A*nd they laughed and laughed and went on laughing
as they picked up the feathers together.